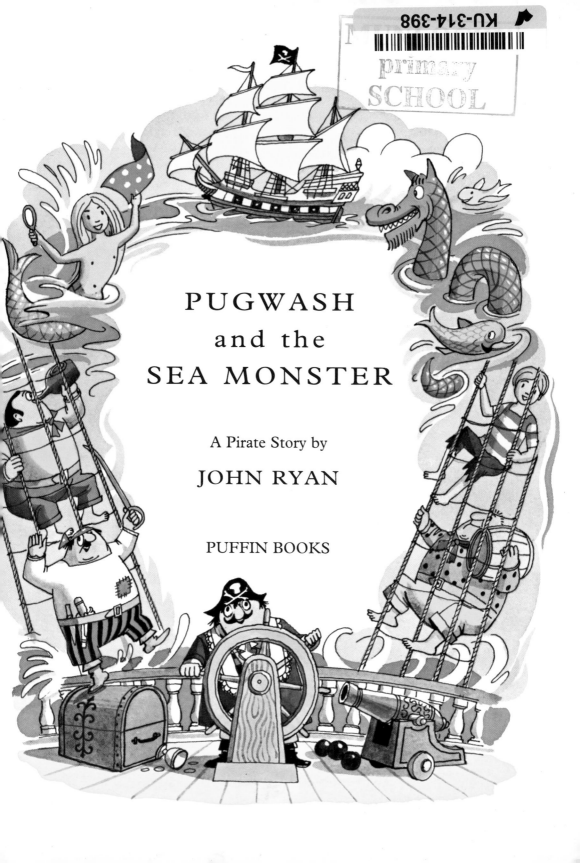

PUGWASH
and the
SEA MONSTER

A Pirate Story by

JOHN RYAN

PUFFIN BOOKS

In an old Spanish fort on Cactus Island in the Caribbean Sea Cut-throat Jake was having a party. It was evening and·he and his ugly crew had brought from their ship a great hoard of treasure to bury in the ruins next day. They ate and drank from the golden plates and goblets and sang and danced and told terrible jokes to each other. They thought of course that nobody knew they were there.

They would not have
been so happy had they
known that close by,
with his ship the *Black
Pig* hidden behind
high rocks . . .

. . . was Captain Pugwash. And
they would have been even
less happy to see, moving
in the shallow water near
the ship, clear against the
setting sun, a most odd-
looking sea monster.
Close up, it looked odder
still.

"Sea Monster, heave to!" came a voice from inside the head.

Then, as the strange creature came to a halt, the head, the hump and the tail lifted up, and there, underneath, were Captain Pugwash, the Mate and Barnabas and Willy.

"Splendid, me hearties!" cried the Captain. "Provided we keep within our depth we cannot fail. Now we can proceed with my plan!"

That night, the pirates held a Council of War. "Now listen very carefully," said the Captain. "Cut-throat Jake is camped in the old Spanish fort with the greatest hoard of treasure in history. We know he is there, but he thinks we are thousands of miles away. Ho-ho—He's got a nasty surprise coming to him!"

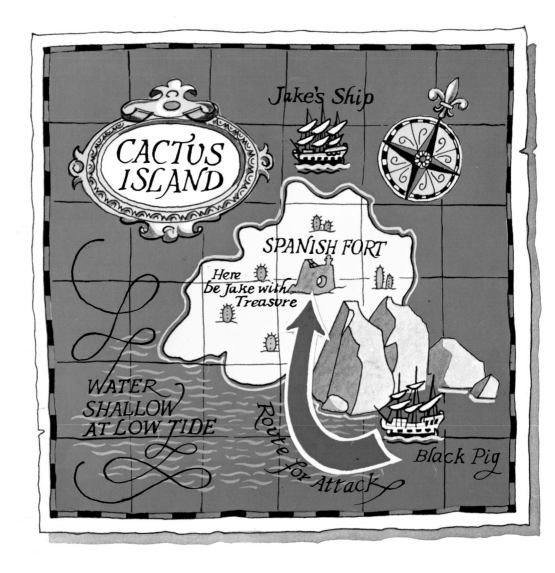

"For at dawn tomorrow, when the tide is low and the water shallow, we shall don our monstrous disguise and advance upon the island. There will be no fighting of course, oh no, nothing as dangerous as that. The very sight of us will terrify Jake and his crew. They'll abandon the treasure, flee to their ship and we, me hearties, we shall all be as rich as kings!"

The pirates were all very excited when they heard the Captain's plan. Only Tom the Cabin-boy didn't seem quite happy about it.

But Pugwash said, "Don't interrupt, Tom, when your elders and betters are speaking. This is my idea and a very clever one, too. We can get along quite well without you. You can stay behind and cook the dinner and mind the ship!"

At first light next day the Captain and his men gathered in the shallow water beside the *Black Pig* and got ready for the great assault.

Pugwash put on the monster's head, the Mate and Barnabas were in the hump—

and Willy wore the tail.

High up in the ruins of
the old fort, Cut-throat
Jake and his men slept
among the cactus plants
and the treasure. They
were all tired out after
a heavy night's eating and
drinking and their snores
were horrible to hear.
Even the lookout . . .

. . . was dozing at his post, until—

"Cap'n Jake! Cap'n Jake!" he yelled. "There's a m-monstrous m-monster down there. It's coming ashore! It'll eat us alive!" In an instant Jake was awake and beside the sentry, swearing terribly. He hated being woken up in the morning.

But when he saw what the
sentry saw, "Creeping catfish,"
he roared. "Run for it! Back
to the ship all of ye! *Run
for your lives!*"

And a moment later, all treasure forgotten, Jake and his crew were dashing in terror from the fort to find their dinghy . . .

. . . while on the other side of the island the 'monster' was arriving, bit by bit on the shore.

"It's worked! My cunning plan has worked!" cried Pugwash. "See! They've gone. They're rowing back to their ship. Hah-hah! What a crafty, capable Captain I am!"

"And—lolloping landlubbers, look at the loot! There's enough booty there to bury a brontosaurus!"

"Very remarkabubble, Cap'n," said the Mate, "but er Cap'n, what about Willy?"

"What do you mean, 'What about Willy'?" retorted the Captain crossly. "Where is he?"

"Look! He's down there," cried Barnabas. "He's still in his tail!"

HELP!

Poor Willy really was in trouble. He was stuck in his tail, he couldn't see where he was going, and the more the Captain shouted at him . . .

. . . the more
muddled
he became.

In the meantime, frightened and weary,
Jake and his men had reached
their own ship.

Up on deck, Jake looked
hurriedly back through his
telescope and saw . . .

. . . first, all by itself, the monster's tail
—and then . . .

"Curses," he roared,
"it's Pugwash!
We've been tricked!
Man the cannon!
We'll blast them off
the face of the island,
then go back for the
treasure!"

But while Jake's pirates were getting
ready to fire, it happened that, attracted
by the sight of the mock monster,

a *real* sea monster, huge, hairy and hideous, was approaching the scene. Jake was so thunderstruck when he saw it that he yelled, "Foiled again!"

"Up anchor! Hoist all sail! Full speed away!" So,
panic stricken and for the second time that day, his
crew rushed and struggled to get their ship moving,
while . . .

... back on the island, Willy had at last unstuck himself and found his way to the others. Captain Pugwash was relieved and delighted to see him, and even more delighted when he saw ...

. . . Jake's ship under full sail being chased far away by the real sea monster. "Tottering turtles! What a fortunate turn of events!" he exclaimed.

"And we'd best be off to the ship, me handsomes, before the creature comes ba for its second course!"

"Ar, but what will we use to carry this little lot off in?" said Barnabas.

"Why, me tail, of course! It'll take it nicely," answered Willy.

"Besides, I'm fond of it now; I'd hate to see it left behind on the island."

So the pirates loaded all the treasure into Willy's
tail, and started to carry it down to the shore. It was
only when they reached the water

that they realised that the water wasn't shallow any more.

In fact, it was far too deep to walk through.

But luckily Tom had been watching, and very soon he was there with the dinghy, just in time to pick up the floundering pirates before they, and the tail full of treasure, sank.

The Captain boasted loudly
[a]s they all towed Willy
[an]d the treasure back
[to]wards the *Black Pig*.

"Kipper me capstans!" he said. "If that wasn't the cleverest, cunningest plan ever!"

"Hm, yes," thought Tom. "It *was* quite a good scheme for once, only I did try to tell him . . .

. . . they'd be out of their depth when the tide came up!''

PUFFIN BOOKS

Published by the Penguin Group: London, New York, Australia, Canada and New Zealand
Penguin Books Ltd, Registered Offices: Harmondsworth, Middlesex, England
First published by The Bodley Head 1976
Published in Puffin Books 1995
3 5 7 9 10 8 6 4 2
Copyright © John Ryan, 1976
All rights reserved
Made and printed in Italy by Printers srl – Trento